POG

For my family: Peter, Stevie, Dom and Jesinda – L.L.
For Bruno with love – K.G.

Scholastic Children's Books,
Commonwealth House, 1-19 New Oxford Street,
London WC1A 1NU, UK
a division of Scholastic Ltd
London ~ New York ~ Toronto ~ Sydney ~ Auckland
Mexico City ~ New Delhi ~ Hong Kong

First published by Omnibus Books, a division of Scholastic Australia, 2000
Published by Scholastic Ltd, 2001

ISBN: 0 439 99395 4

POG

By Lyn Lee
Illustrated by Kim Gamble

Hippo

 Pog lived with his mum, who was as busy as a dung beetle, and his dad, who was often away on mysterious business.

There was baby Bedlam, who didn't do much of anything yet, and Nanna, who sat and talked to her pet pot plants.

And there was big brother Vandal.

Pog was as brave as a bathtub full of sharks. He was afraid of nothing … well, nothing very much. It was only at bedtime, when shadows play tricks on the eyes, that Pog grew nervous.

"Better check under the bed for children," crooned Vandal, and he softly laughed his wicked laugh.

"I'm two metres tall and older than I have ever been," said Pog. "I'm not afraid of anything!"

 But he was.

He was very afraid of children.

Every night he checked
carefully under his bed,

inside the toybox,

and behind the door.

Then he would sneak up to his wardrobe and wrench the door open. Everybody knows that's where children like to hide most.

 He kept his night light on and pulled the covers up tight under his chin until he fell asleep.

 **W**hen he woke up in the morning he bounced out of bed full of bedbugs. He had made it through another night.

 When Pog started school, he had to walk with Vandal.

"I am two metres tall and older than I have ever been. I can walk to school by myself," Pog said to his mum.

"Not yet," she smiled.

 "Pog's too little to walk by himself," crooned Vandal as they set off for school.

"I'm as brave as a bucketful of snails," said Pog, and he stuck out his lip in a terrifying pout. "I don't need you."

 "What about children hiding along the way?" Vandal growled.

Pog was shocked. He thought children only came out when it was dark, like a night mist, or a bad dream.

Vandal grinned his wicked grin.

"They wait in the bushes until a little monster comes wandering alone," he said. "Then they leap out and pack you in a sack and drag you away. So stick with me, or you'll be in trouble!"

 Pog stuck with Vandal all day.

 On their way home they heard a whimpering and wailing, a groaning and moaning.

Pog stopped. He grabbed Vandal.

 "It's children!" squeaked Pog. "Children in the bushes!"

"Don't be stupid," growled Vandal. "There's no such thing."

Vandal parted the bushes, and there, stuck among some thorny branches, eyes wide and wet, nose red and running, and mouth open in a black, high-pitched wail, was … a child.

Vandal went white with shock. He shook with fear.

Then he fled down the road without looking back.

Pog thought he must be dreaming. He stood and looked at the child. It was so small, so sad and so damp that he couldn't be afraid of it.

"Who are you?" asked Pog. "What's wrong?"

"My name is Tom and I'm having a bad dream and I can't wake up," said the child.

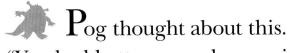 Pog thought about this.
"You had better come home with me," he said.

The family was flummoxed when Pog turned up with Tom.

Mum cowered in the corner, clutching Bedlam to her breast.

Dad thought Tom was a nightmare and tried to catch him in his net.

 Nanna told Tom
to get back to his pot –
she thought he was a plant.

And Vandal stood quivering
and quaking, shivering and
shaking.

Pog said, "He has to stay.
I have to dream him away."

Pog went to bed early that night. He didn't check under his bed, or inside the toybox, or behind the door.

Instead, he told Tom to sit in the wardrobe.

"Everybody knows that's where children hide, ready to jump out and scare little monsters," explained Pog.

Pog fell asleep. He dreamed of children. Children
laughing in the playground, children playing in the sun.
But he wasn't scared.

He dreamed of Tom running home, where his parents were waiting.

When Pog woke up next morning, he jumped out of bed full of bedbugs.

He opened the wardrobe door.

Tom was gone.

 Pog was as brave as a barrel full of worms. "I am two metres tall and older than I have ever been," he said.

And he was never, ever afraid of anything again.

Well, not very much.